Tales of the Lying Nutcracker

Tales of the Lying Nutcracker

Written and illustrated by

Janosch

Translated by Erika Hyams

A Grasshopper Book

Abelard-Schuman

London

ISBN 0 200 72036 8 (Paperback)

ISBN 0 200 72035 X (Hardback)

Abelard-Schuman
450 Edgware Road,
London W2

24 Market Square
Aylesbury, Buckinghamshire

Printed in Great Britain

IBM Computer Typesetting by Print Origination. Liverpool

1. **About Inky-Punch who had ears like sails, the Teddybear who played the fiddle, and the broken dog who could not stop crying, and also about the Lying Nutcracker, Lari Fari Tricktooth, and John the Lion.**

In Number 11 North Alley, high up under the roof and behind the seventh rafter in the house where Mr. Railman the old chief railway signalman lived, stood a very mysterious box. It looked exactly like a treasure chest and, what is more, it was exactly the same colour as a treasure chest. Even more remarkable, it was exactly the same size as a treasure chest—if not a little larger. But at one corner where the lid didn't fit tightly, a lion's paw peeped out.

Moreover, when the moon shone through the window at half-past nine each evening, something very, very odd happened.

The lid began to move.

And somebody looked out.

Somebody lifted the lid and looked around.

Somebody shook his head and

stretched his legs, and then climbed out of the chest and sat down on the very edge of the rim.

It was Lari Fari Tricktooth. Then he began to sing:

Wake up my friends, and listen to me,
And I'll tell you a marvellous history,

Some adventure of mine—Oh, what
  could be stranger?
A tale of magic, of adventure and
  danger.
I'm Tricktooth the Nutcracker. Come
  open your eyes!
My stories are true, for I tell you no
  lies!

And there was Lari Fari Tricktooth
himself, the Lying Nutcracker, who had
interchangeable sets of teeth all of which
he used to tell lies. He had lion's teeth,
teeth to crack giant stones with, fox-
catching teeth and a hundred other sets
which he had been able to use on various
occasions, but which had been stolen by
the robber Whizzbung—or so he said. His
peppermill teeth fell from the bridge into
a river eleven years ago during a storm.
At least, that's what he said—unless he
was lying.

Lari Fari had hardly finished singing
before all the other toy people came out
of the mysterious box and sprang to life.
They climbed over each other, sat on the
edge of the chest and made themselves
comfortable.

First, as always, was Inky-Punch, with

ears that stood so high that on a windy day he needed only to stand in a field to be blown away up into the sky. He could win a competition with house-martins hands down! Inky-Punch was a silly old chatterbox who always interrupted other people.

Then came the fiddler, the Teddybear with his violin. He played so well that he could make the broken dog with only three legs and no tail cry whenever he played.

The rubber-duck came next, followed by the floppy stuffed puppet, a porcelain doll with curly hair, and the old crocodile Bimbanfiddleraddle and his baby Bimbanfiddleraddlekin.

Last of all came the truthful lion John, with his honest eyes. Honest John the Lion had never ever told a lie! He was stronger than all the other toy people and had teeth so sharp that he could eat them all up. It was John the Lion who made sure that nobody told any lies.

Every evening, when the toy people were sitting on the edge of the chest, Honest John put his head on his paws and said, "Come on, Lari Fari Tricktooth, tell us a story. But if you tell a lie,

8

and your story isn't the honest truth,
then I shall eat you up like a woodworm.
Honestly!"

And every evening at half-past nine,
the Nutcracker, Lari Fari Tricktooth, told
them a new story.

2. How Lari Fari Tricktooth was a miller, and how he caught the famous pickpocket Freddy Fleshfinger, just as he tried to steal a bird.

"Once upon a time I was a miller," began Lari Fari one evening, "in the beautiful toy-chest country of Suck-a-sweet. Actually the people of that country had nothing to eat because there was no wind, so that the sails of the windmill stood still. They couldn't grind their corn, you see, for, as the proverb says, where there is no wind there is no flour. The people might have starved to death—but that's where I came in.

"I stretched and stretched and made myself remarkably tall. People brought long ladders and leaned them up against me. Then they carried their sacks of grain up the ladders and poured it all between my teeth. At that time I was wearing my flour-milling teeth and I ground their flour so fine that they could bake cakes with it and eat them all day long. I can tell you that that is no lie! They were cakes with icing sugar on top and raisins inside. Why, I became so full of flour that it even came out of my back and the

farmhands had to put it into sacks."

"Is that the truth?" growled Honest John. "Is that the honest truth? If you are lying, I shall hit you with my paw, honestly!"

"It's honestly true," said Lari Fari Tricktooth, turning round. "Have a good look at my back. There's flour there still!" Sure enough, a little flour was trickling down his back—but actually it came from a woodworm!

"Good!" growled Honest John. "That's right! It's not a lie. Carry on with the story."

"So I became a very respected person, and everybody knew me. It just so happened that the famous pickpocket Freddy Fleshfinger was around at that time, and nothing was safe from him. Nobody managed to catch him out, and nobody knew the tricks he got up to. The police didn't even know what he looked like because he was clever and disguised himself in the most cunning ways. Sometimes he went about without a cap, and at other times without a hat—or he went without his false moustache. Once he went without whiskers so that people became quite confused—but then I came along! I'm much cleverer than the police.

"As you know, a pickpocket is much more difficult to catch than an ordinary thief. He doesn't steal from kitchens, or bedrooms and sitting-rooms where a simple trap would be enough to catch him. No, a pickpocket goes about his business craftily.

"You might be standing at a vegetable stall in the market, wanting to buy something nice like a pound or two of fruit or a bag of peanuts, when somebody sidles up to you, stands next to you, grins a little, waves one hand about, and wrinkles up his nose like Inky-Punch with an earwig in his pocket.

"You look at him and think, 'What a friendly man!' but while you are doing this—snap! His free hand has pulled out of your pocket your lovely packet of ham sandwiches, and you put your hand in it) without your even noticing it. He moves away, you gaze after him, and perhaps even wave to him in a friendly fashion and wish him all the best—and in no time at all he has disappeared from sight. Then you sit down on a box of tomatoes, looking forward to eating your ham sandwiches, and you put your hand

in your jacket pocket—and it's empty!
You've got nothing to eat! That's the
mean sort of thing a pickpocket does.
But then, as I said, I came along!"

"I once knew somebody," said Inky-
Punch, "who wanted to put his hand in
his pocket to get out his sandwiches, but
he hadn't got any because he. . . ."

Teddybear, the violinist, quickly hit
him over the head with his bow to
quieten him down, and Inky-Punch immediately fell silent.

"And so I went to the weekly market and stood inconspicuously by the stall of the birdseller, Jacob, and pretended to buy a little bird. I didn't really buy one. I just pretended to put one in my back trouser pocket, but instead of a little bird I put my knife-sharp fox-catching teeth in it. And so, at the same time that I thrust my fox-catchers teeth in the pocket, I started to whistle through my teeth at the same time, very quietly and beautifully—just like a little bird, like a canary. I could always whistle like an expert . . .."

"If you tell a fib," growled Honest John the Lion, "I shall give you one on the nose with my paw! Come on, whistle for us." The Lying Nutcracker moved his one moveable leg so that it squeaked. A lion, of course, doesn't understand much about music, for he himself can only grumble and growl, and so Honest John rumbled, "Good! Sounds beautiful. Carry on with the story."

"The thief approached," the Lying Nutcracker went on, "thinking, 'Aha! He has bought a little bird for himself.' He came nearer and stood on my right side and started to wave his hands about, just like the ears of a hare. He smiled at me. I looked innocent and just watched him. In the meantime he put his long pickpocket fingers stealthily into my back trouser pocket, and as he did so—whoosh! I snapped him up with my fox-catching teeth. The scoundrel was caught! And then he started to whimper!

"The police came and took him to jail, and I pocketed the reward of seven hundred trouser buttons and bought myself lots of nuts with them—three different kinds! It's the honest truth!"

"That's right," growled Honest John the Lion, "there *are* three kinds of nuts—hazelnuts, walnuts and Welsh anthracite nuts. It's true all right. If that rascal had lied, I would have eaten him up—with icing sugar and apple sauce."

3. How Lari Fari Tricktooth came to be employed to count the shooting stars in the town of Wurmerlitz and had a quarrel with the moon.

"Once upon a time," began Lari Fari Tricktooth, "I was employed in the beautiful town of Wurmerlitz, not as a nightwatchman or a street-sweeper or anything like that, but as a counter of shooting stars. 'He who has sharp teeth also has keen eyes' is a well-known proverb among birds."

"Sometimes I actually think," purred Honest John the Lion, "that he isn't a liar at all, for I know that proverb myself. I for one have sharp teeth and keen eyes. What he says is quite right."

"Every day—that is, every night, I mean," went on Lari Fari Tricktooth, "I had to go on my rounds and walk through the streets and count the shooting stars in the sky.

"The famous Professor Noddlehead collected the number of shooting stars over the whole country and sent them by express messenger to America. There the numbers of shooting stars from the whole world were added up and put in front of

17

the President—and then the President could do whatever he liked with them. As you all know, anybody who sees a shooting star can have a wish, so the person who has added up *all* the shooting stars in the whole world—let's say three million, for instance—well, he can have three million wishes. What a lucky fellow!"

"That's right," growled the Honest Lion, "he's a lucky chap, honestly!"

"All right, then," continued the Lying Nutcracker. "The moon used to light up for me while I was working. Every night he arrived punctually and rose behind my house, and together we went on my rounds. Mind you, he didn't do it for nothing. Once a week I polished him until he shone."

"Aha! Now he's lying," growled Honest John the Lion, "because that's just not possible. No one can polish the moon. There are mountains on the moon, and nobody can polish mountains. This will probably cost you your life, my good fellow! But still, I'll just let you finish this story. The more you lie, the better you'll taste, honestly!"

"Then suddenly one night," Lari Fari Tricktooth went on, "he didn't appear. I waited in front of the house, time went by. I should have started to count already, for the shooting stars were falling from the sky in a shower—but the villain didn't come. I went down the garden to meet him, but he wasn't there. I guessed at the number of shooting stars and entered them in my account book—four hundred and ninety-three, I remember. He didn't turn up the next night either. I began to get angry with him. He hadn't come by nine o'clock, nor by ten o'clock or even eleven o'clock. So, when he still hadn't come on the following night, I went out onto the roofs to look for him. Then I saw him! He was hiding behind the water tower, the coward.

"I raced down from the roof at a gallop, rushed through the streets, right up to the water tower, and climbed up on it. And there he sat, all right, but he was *below* me by now. I could have jumped down on him, but he's round—or, at least, he *was* round—and I might have slipped off him and broken something. So then I had to coax him in a cunning sort of way . . .."

"In Wetborough, where I come from," said Inky-Punch, "we have a water tower

too, but the water tower in Wet-borough. . . ."

Bang! Teddybear the Fiddler hit the chatterbox with his bow right on the back of the head so that he stopped gabbling immediately.

". . . to come up to me. I spoke softly to him, and began to whistle gently to him, but he still wouldn't come. So then I allowed myself just one small lie. I said to him, 'If you don't want to shine for me, you don't need to. It's all right. I'll go home.' But I didn't actually go home.

"I hid on top of the tower behind the balustrade and waited. Everything worked out just as I had planned. The moon climbed up in a leisurely sort of way, and when he stood just as high as the water tower and there wasn't a fraction of an inch between us, I grabbed his trousers with my teeth, and held on to them tightly. Although I only wanted to make him shine for me, he began to quarrel with me straight away. He called me a nit-picker, a twaddler. He even called me stiff-leg and woodworm-sandwich. Of course, we had a furious fight after that and somehow, during it, I must have bitten too hard, for all of a sudden I bit a piece out of his behind. And that was that! It's the honest truth, that is!"

"But it's a lie!" growled the Honest Lion John. "Now it's all up with you this time, you liar. I saw the moon last week, and he was all there." John the Honest Lion came nearer and used his paw to wipe the dust off the Lying Nutcracker's hat. "That's so that you'll taste better, my friend. . . ."

He was just going to gobble him up when Lari Fari Tricktooth shouted, "Turn round first quickly, friend lion. What can you see?"

The Honest Lion swung round and caught sight of the moon through the skylight. Thinking there must be something wrong with his sight, he climbed quickly down from the chest and went up to the pane of glass and put his paws on the edge of it. Sure enough, a piece was missing from the moon. "It's true," he growled. "He hasn't told a lie. Sometimes I think he lies and sometimes I think that he doesn't. He makes me quite confused, the rascal, honestly he does."

The toy people climbed back into their

box and Inky-Punch said, "Do you know
a story about a fox, Lari Fari Tricktooth?
You see, in Wetborough we had. . . ."
Teddybear the Fiddler struck him over

the nose with his bow, making a lovely
sound which reverberated all round the
room long after all the toy people from
the chest had fallen asleep.

4. A story about a trained set of fox-catching teeth, the fox in the field, and the beautiful Princess Lulu of Marzipan.

"As it happens, I know a story about a fox," began Lari Fari the Nutcracker with the Lying Teeth, "because I know beautiful stories about everything—and they are all absolutely true.

"I used to have twenty-four sets of teeth, all interchangeable, at one time. One of them was my fox-trapping set which became so famous that stories about them appeared in hunting magazines.

"So, therefore, I was not surprised when a postcard arrived one day sent by King Baldrian of France. His Christian name was Louis, as it happens. He wrote to tell me that they had a fox in their woods who was so clever that no one could catch him. The King went on to say that this fox was so cunning that he led all the hunters by their nose—or misled them, if you see what I mean—and that no gun was accurate enough to hit him and so on.

"Well, now, as you know, I have a lot

25

of free time at Whitsun, for nobody eats nuts then and there isn't any work for me to do. I used to spend this time to take my false teeth outside the town where I put them into training, for they had to keep fit. Sometimes I threw stones and made them go and look for them:

> 'Katy, spring for me,
> Katy bring to me
> The pebble, I beg.
> Show a leg! Show a leg!'

"I trained them the way humans train their dogs. I made them jump over sticks and taught them to sing, to perform double somersaults and to dog-paddle in

the water. In short, I taught them all the tricks dogs can be taught. My fox-catching teeth were the most successful. They were best at following a trail and picking up a scent, at standing up on their hind legs, at coming to heel—they could do almost anything. I could have performed in a circus with my fox-catching teeth. Now that isn't a lie!"

"Where we lived in Wetborough," babbled Inky-Punch, "there was a man once and he had a dog who. . . ." Yet again Teddybear the Violinist hit him over the head with his bow because Inky-Punch never stops babbling once he has started. He babbles and babbles all through the night, and tomorrow, and the day after tomorrow, and the whole of next week until somebody taps him on the head. Only then does he stop.

"To continue. The address was on the postcard and so I went to France to hunt the fox. We posted ourselves (and there were over a hundred of us) all around the wood. The fox couldn't possibly escape, we thought. The wood was carefully combed right the way through it, every leaf was turned, sticks were used to poke into every possible hole, the bushes were beaten—but still there was no fox.

"I wasn't bothered, for my teeth hadn't yet picked up the trace of a scent yet. They were in the pocket of my jacket and were absolutely silent. By this time the hunt was coming to an end, and King Louis Baldrian of France was as red as a beetroot. At last the chief huntsman blew his horn—the fox had got away!

"That's where I came in. When all the hunters had assembled in front of the wood, the King said, 'I shall give my beautiful daughter, Lulu of Marzipan, as the wife of whoever catches the fox.' Suddenly I felt my fox-catching teeth in my pocket becoming restless. They had caught the scent of the fox. They had got wind of the rascal!"

"That's true," said the rubber-duck. "The fox *is* a rascal. He gobbles up chickens and young ducks. He's a scoundrel and a vagabond, right enough."

"If that is true," thought Honest John the Lion, "then it is not a lie. If it isn't a lie, then I can't eat him up—but *if* he lies, he's going to catch it, honestly!"

"Suddenly the fox appeared and sat in the middle of the field out of the range of the guns. He had got away through an underground tunnel, and he waved his paw at us. He grinned too, because he thought no gun could possibly shoot that far—and he was right. I could have sent my fox-catching teeth after him but by the time they got there, he would have been far away and over the hills. But I was clever. I took my fox-catching teeth out of my pocket with my right hand and threw them as close to the villain as I could—and they landed only two inches away. Before he had time to think, my teeth had caught him by the tail! I shouted:

> 'Katy, spring for me,
> Katy bring to me
> Thc pcbble, I beg.
> Show a leg! Show a leg!'

"And so they brought me the fox alive. He was put into chains and kept as

a prisoner of King Louis Baldrian of France for the rest of his days—and that's no lie!"

"And what happened to the beautiful Princess Lulu of Marzipan, friend Nutcracker?" asked Teddybear the Violinist. "Did you receive her hand in marriage?" The old, sweet-toothed bear liked stories about Princesses and dolls best of all.

"She gave me her hand and we became man and wife. Tomorrow I shall tell you the story of our wedding," said Lari Fari Tricktooth the Lying Nutcracker—for he only told one story each night and he had finished the story about the fox-hunt.

5. A story about how Lari Fari Tricktooth married the beautiful Princess Lulu of Marzipan, and about all the good things there were to eat at the wedding, and also about the children of Marzipan.

"We had our wedding on a Wednesday," said Lari Fari Tricktooth the next night. "I remember exactly when it was, because Wednesday has always been my favourite day of the week ever since I was a baby nutcracker. My father, you see, used to come to visit us on Wednesdays and we always had ginger nuts for lunch. I love ginger nuts, they are my second favourite food. It used to be lovely. . . ." The Lying Nutcracker was feeling homesick, and it was so quiet in the chest that you could have heard the woodworm who lived in his trousers coughing loudly.

"People who are homesick don't lie," thought Honest John the Lion. "That is a proverb, and proverbs are really true if they are not lies."

"Well, then, I took her hand in marriage. That is, she was made my wife. I mean, she celebrated the wedding with

32

me. A wedding is an occasion where everyone from the toy-chest is invited. We had music—music made by the humming top, and a violin-playing bear, and a monkey playing an accordion.

"The guests ate and drank to their hearts' content. We fried four hundred and three nut cutlets and four hundred and two portions of walnut roast. We had five bathtubs of coconut milk—hazelnut flavour—and the clockwork monkey gave a concert on the jingling piano, pushing the pedals really hard.

"My beautiful Marzipan Princess, the rose of my heart, Lulu, smelled like a flower. She didn't leave my side. She clung to me. She was as close to me as one potato is to another when they are stored for the winter. Whenever she touched me it was a bit like being tickled by an electric current. My wood nearly caught fire. It certainly smouldered quite a bit."

"What a liar!" growled the Honest Lion John. "That's utterly impossible."
"Let's see the proof—if there is any."

The Lying Nutcracker lifted his movable leg and showed a burn mark. (Once, at Christmas-time, a candle had fallen on to it—but nobody knew about that.)

"Right," growled the Honest Lion. "What burns makes burn marks. There is a proverb that says so—and proverbs are true, if they aren't lies, that is."

"Well, then," continued the Lying Nutcracker, "we had a lovely party. My father-in-law, the King of France, gave us a wedding present of a little box that had a lock on it—only one lock, but it had two keys. We lived in it and always kept it locked from the inside. That was the happiest time of my life. It was always dark inside, and it was so small that we were always rather squashed. That was a lazy time, friends. All we did was to shake a bit when a train went by.

"We had two hundred and seventy children, each blacker than the next, because it was always so dark in the box—black nut-marzipan children, they were. But I haven't heard anything of any of them for some time. They emigrated. Blown to the four winds, they were. At least twenty-five of them moved to a sweetshop in Pontefract where they disappeared one after the other. I expect that they all got married as well."

"I should like to get married too," growled the Honest Lion, "only I don't quite know who to."

6. How Lari Fari Tricktooth saved the toy-chest people and chased away the Pepper Dwarfs by beating them with their own weapons.

"The nastiest dwarfs in the whole world are the Pepper Dwarfs who come from mouseholes, and I shall tell you why they are so nasty straight away," began Lari Fari Tricktooth.

"First of all I loathe them, because they chase the nice little mice out of their holes so that they can settle in them themselves and make themselves confortable. That way they don't have to do any work like digging holes; one should never chase people who are weaker or hit them or make fun of them. Secondly, I think they are nasty because they are deceitful, and thirdly, I can't bear them anyway. Now I'll tell you why. They don't wash, and they smell and they tell lies—and, as you know, I can't stand liars.

"The Pepper Dwarfs are a little smaller than those little woollen hedgehogs you sometimes see in toy-chests and they are as strong as fully grown billy goats, although they smell a hundred times worse. They are grey all over and have moustaches as big as children's toothbrushes, although you can hardly see them at all. They live on pepper, and look like human beings, but they are really very tiny.

"They invade one toyland after another. They crush peppercorns with teeth which are as sharp as flint, and then they blow pepper into the eyes of the dolls to make them cry. Sometimes they come along with a kindly air and stroke the dolls and pretend to comfort them, and then—bang! They gobble the poor things up, nicely spiced with pepper, of course.

"Naturally they can't eat me up, because I'm made of wood, and so I shouldn't taste particularly nice. Anyway, a thousand Pepper Dwarfs can't beat me in strength and cunning. Now I shall tell you how I conquered them. At the time I was living in the toyland of Suck-a-sweet."

"I don't believe it. He's telling a lie," rumbled John the Honest Lion. "No real country can have such a silly name."

''Six toy-boxes belonged to our country, and all of them were full to the brim," went on the Lying Nutcracker, "and then quite suddenly, the peace was

disturbed. Someone had seen the Pepper
Dwarfs creeping along and hiding behind
the barrier at the frontier! Somebody else
had actually seen them sharpening their
teeth and drinking special aiming-water
by the gallon. They drink this so that
they can aim the peppercorns more
accurately. They had already collected
mountains of peppercorns and piled them
up so that they were five hundred yards
high."

"Now, honestly, you're telling whop-
pers!" roared the Honest Lion John, running his tongue over his teeth and moving

a little nearer to the edge of the chest. "Five hundred yards is too high!"

"Honestly, it isn't a lie," cried Tricktooth the Lying Nutcracker, "and if you will only wait until I get to the end of the story I shall prove that it's absolutely true. Well, then, there was a tumult in our toy-chest country—just like there is at the annual world-famous funfair in Parsleybed in Russia. The people polished their weapons, and gave their trumpets a shine, and then they poured oil into the pianos and blew air into Frank the Monkey's concertina."

"If you are trying to tell us that trumpets are weapons," growled John the Honest Lion, "then I shall have to put you right. What you are saying is ridiculously silly. But still, since it's only one stupid little lie, I shan't hold it against you—yet. We'll see what happens later on!"

"Well, then," said Lari Fari Tricktooth, "I had taken command, and then I issued an order. All stuffed dolls and all little toys less than two inches high had to go into the wooden box decorated with iron nails. I took up my position in

the middle of the square with the jumping tin frogs on either side of me, so that there was one rank to the right and one to the left. The Pepper Dwarfs attacked. The tin frogs were meant to jump on their necks and throw those rascals to the ground if anything happened to me. I had put on my peppermill teeth, for I thought that it is always easier to beat an enemy with his own weapons. And that was. . . ."

"Pepper! That's what it was," began Inky-Punch, the chatterbox, once again. "Once where I lived in. . . ."

The teddybear lifted up his bow and was just about to hit him on the head when Inky-Punch, spotting it, suddenly stopped babbling.

"For instance," the Lying Nutcracker continued, "I once got the better of a liar by treating him to a dose of his own lies. Tomorrow I'll tell you the story of the Fiddle-Faddle, the Master Liar, and then you'll see.

"Anyway, when the peppercorns were flying through the air, I caught them with my teeth, ground them up, and blew them straight back at the Pepper Dwarfs. And what I expected actually happened!

41

They couldn't take their own pepper—especially in the eyes. They turned tail and ran off, and were never seen again. Now, my friends, I shall prove to you that my story is true." Lari Fari Tricktooth turned round. "See those holes," he said. "They are the marks where the peppercorns hit me." (Of course, really they were woodworm holes.)

"They're woodworm holes, you ruffian!" exclaimed John the Honest Lion. "Now you'll take a long holiday, my friend," he growled. "Take off your boots so that it is easier to eat you up!"

"No, no!" cried Lari Fari Tricktooth. "I shall prove that I haven't been lying. Look here, you've got a brain in your head, haven't you?"

"Yes—much better than a big-game hunter's!"

"Well, then, tell me. Have you ever seen a Pepper Dwarf?"

"Never," said Honest John the Lion. "Not even from behind."

"And why not? I'll tell you. It's because they have gone. And why have they gone? Because I chased them off, that's why. Otherwise they wouldn't have gone, now would they? Well, then, if you are going to say that I'm telling lies and that you have seen Pepper Dwarfs after all, then you are nothing but a liar yourself. Now then, friend lion, are you going to eat me up?"

"He's right," growled Honest John the Lion. "I *would* be a liar myself then—but I'm not. Honestly I'm not."

"If I wanted to," said Lari Fari Tricktooth, "I could lie like mad. However, tomorrow I'll tell you the story of how I happened to meet the Chief of all Liars, Fiddle-Faddle Flyfeet—and you shall hear how I managed to get the better of him."

7. **How Lari Fari Tricktooth trapped the Chief of the Liars, Fiddle-Faddle Flyfeet, and won the Order of the Trouser Pocket of Fool's Gold with Diamonds.**

"You can recognise liars," said Lari Fari Tricktooth, "by the way they wear their hats on the sides of their heads. They like to dress up in beautiful clothes and wear cheap tin ornaments. Now once I actually beat the Master Liar Fiddle-Faddle Flyfeet in a lying competition. But I must tell you the story from the beginning, for it's a really good one.

"At this time I was already more famous than . . . well, than an opera singer, for instance. My name was in the telephone directory and a man in Africa read about me. His name was actually Mr. Buckshot. He sent me an airmail letter asking me to join him on a lion hunt. He wanted me to bite a few lions. . . ."

"To bite *what*?" growled Honest John the Lion. "I didn't quite catch it. Did you say 'lions'?"

"To bite—er—li-ti," said the Lying Nutcracker quickly. "I mean, ligers that is to say, tigers, simply tigers. I've never

45

attacked lions. Lions are my friends. I like them so much. They have such lovely soft fur—outside, anyway. Inside they are hard—in the teeth, I mean."

"I can assure you of that," rumbled Honest John the Lion. "Come here and feel."

"No, thank you," said Tricktooth the Lying Nutcracker, hastily. "I must carry on with my story. I travelled for four years and three months exactly, on foot all the way, through the desert with the sun above and sand underfoot and me in the middle without any water. I had such a thirst! I thought my wood was going to catch fire.

"I think I must have lost my way, for I had no compass with me. Suddenly I came to a city that looked like Jerusalem. All round me there were hundreds, no, thousands—no, hundreds of thousands of people, and they were all there because the Champion Liar, Fiddle-Faddle Flyfeet, was challenging the best liars in the world to a contest of three kinds: simple lying; double lying; acute-angled, three-cornered, direct cheating and downright lying, backwards and forwards, by heart and without a book.

"By the time that I arrived, two hundred and eleven champion liars had already been beaten and had given up. Fiddle-Faddle Flyfeet the Master Liar was a clear winner on points. Nobody dared to challenge him again.

"But then I turned up. The referee was a desert fish with and without wings—"

"This time, brother liar, you really are going to be my prey!" growled John the Honest Liar. "As sure as a flea in a baboon, I shall eat you up without even calling for pepper and salt. I'm an expert on desert animals—and there aren't any desert fish." John the Honest Lion sidled a few inches closer and rubbed his paws together.

"In the market place," continued Lari Fari the Lying Nutcracker quickly, "stood the Master Liar Fiddle-Faddle Flyfeet who lied so much that he made my braces burst. The desert-braces-lying-referee-flying-fish asked me my name. I told him it was Lari Fari Tricktooth, and when he asked my profession, I said that I was a very strong nutcracker, born in the toyland of Suck-a-sweet."

"I shall eat you up, wood, woodworm and all!" growled Honest John the Lion happily, moving closer still.

"And then the lying-desert-braces-presiding-desert-fish told me that it was my turn and that I had to tell some lies.

"So I began: 'Well, then, yesterday I was walking across the sea, without luggage, just strolling along, when I suddenly had an itch in the tooth. I thought to myself that it was just a grain of sand but it was, in fact, half a nutshell from the two thousand or so nuts I crack each day. I spat it out and then looked inside it. There was a huge desert. I could see a steamer with a crew of a thousand men floating in the desert. It was floating quite peacefully. The helmsman was my friend the monkey, Ignatius, who comes from the same toybox. I was very keen to go up to him and shake his paw—but then the sun in my nutshell went down and set in the east. I fell over the railings and drowned in the sand.' "

"This time, you villain, I've got you! I've got you as sure as my tail's at the other end," roared the Honest Lion John. "The sun sets in the west, you false tooth!"

"All the people clapped like anything," Lari Fari Tricktooth went on. "They called out, 'Wonderful! Fantastic lying! He's not in the same class as Fiddle-Faddle Flyfeet, though.'

"Then it was Fiddle-Faddle Flyfeet's turn. 'Well lied,' he said, 'for I remember exactly that tomorrow I shall plant a tiny little nut tree in a little pot no bigger than a thimble. It must be from this tree that your little nuts all must have come. Now it's your turn again, Mr. Tricktooth.'

"Quickly I said, 'What Mr. Fiddle-Faddle Flyfeet says is quite true.'

"And then Fiddle-Faddle Flyfeet shouted, 'What do you mean? You say it's true? I've never told the truth in my life. What an impertinent liar you are. That's the biggest lie I've ever heard!'

"I had trapped Fiddle-Faddle Flyfeet, my friends! After all, he said himself that he'd never heard a bigger lie!"

"And that's exactly what *I* say too," growled the Honest Lion to the Lying Nutcracker, wiping his mouth with his paw. "And now I'm going to eat you up. Crrrunch! Crrrunch!"

"But I said myself that I'm the biggest liar," cried Lari Fari Tricktooth. "And that's the truth, isn't it? Do you want to eat someone just because he's told the truth, Honest John?"

"Oh, no, not at all. If I did, I think he would stick in my throat, honestly!" said Honest John the Lion hastily.

"Well, then, that's true enough, since you don't lie yourself. So you can't eat me then. What I must add, though, is that I was awarded the Order of the Trouser Pocket for Double Liars in three classes, gilded back and front, and studded with diamonds. I'm telling you the truth, all right. It's fool's gold, and it's hall-marked."

8. How the three robbers, Eeny, Meeny and the Fat Caramba wanted to attack Toyland and how Lari Fari Tricktooth took them prisoner.

"Once I conquered the three most famous robbers in all the toy-chest countries. First there was Eeny, then Meeny, and then there was the Fat Caramba.

"At the time there lived in our toy-chest country a number of little jelly babies. There was a whole suitcase full. They were all sisters and each as beautiful as the other. Now robbers were after them, for robbers love jelly babies."

"That's true," began Inky-Punch. "In Wctborough where I was born there lived a really wild robber called Bimban, and he needed a little sugar doll every day before his lunch. Without it his robber-dinner wouldn't taste right, and so. . . ."

Here Teddybear the Fiddler hit him on his cap with his fiddle and Inky-Punch immediately stopped babbling.

"I am even cleverer than the police," said Lari Fari Tricktooth, "because I am bigger. What is more, I am also cleverer than clockwork King January of Suck-a-sweet who owns a tin crown and wears lacquered shoes.

"Well, a wooden bird brought the news that the three robbers, Eeny, Meeny and the Fat Caramba, were on their way from the neighbouring toy-chest land and that they were clearly making for our suitcase full of jelly babies. Since the three of them could easily have carried the case away with them, our people were terribly afraid.

"And that's where I came in—what with my sharp intellect, my forty-eight interchangeable sets of teeth, and the fast leg on one side which is so strong that I could use it to kick the moon into goal, just like a football. I posted myself inconspicuously inside a shoe-box right next to

the door, since that was where the frontier of our toy-chest land was.

"Then night came. It was so dark that I couldn't see my own leg in front of my nose. Suddenly I heard two footsteps behind the door. Clever fellow that I am, I had posted one set of teeth on the right side of this door and another set on the left. Then there was another next to the set on the right, and another next to the set on the left, and again, another on the right and one on the left and so on. The villains came nearer and nearer."

"I believe him," growled John the Honest Lion. "I know that right and left really *do* exist. Right is here, and left is there. In front is in front, and at the back I have a tail. Only I'm not quite sure which paw is on the left, but I think that the left is on the right and the right is on the left. Therefore it's just possible that the Nutcracker isn't really a liar after all."

"And then I heard the door squeak," said Lari Fari Tricktooth. "A hard, robber's boot creaked. There came the sound of another footstep. Then the Fat Caramba coughed and said, 'I haven't had a jelly baby between my teeth for a long time now. It will taste marvellous, won't it, my robber-friends? I hope you haven't forgotten your pepper and salt. We'll have to flavour them. Ha, ha, ha!'

"Suddenly my fox-catchers started making a grinding noise behind him. It was only a slight noise, but I knew the robbers were startled. As they turned to the left my lion-catching teeth snapped behind them on the right. . . ."

"Your *what*? What did you say?" growled Honest John. "Lion's what? I didn't quite catch it. . . ."

"Li—lini—lino—linoleum teeth to bite linoleum with, I mean. Then, all at once there were sets of teeth snapping away behind the robbers—first on the left, and then the right. One set whistled loudly. Another snapped robber Eeny on the seat of his trousers. The thieves thought that they were surrounded. They started to shake so much that a lid of a box fell down and bent a tin soldier's rifle. Then they started to run as if the police were after them. My fox-catchers caught Meeny by his hands, handcuffing him. Eeny wanted to help him, but my fox-catchers quickly snapped together again and so grabbed both robbers at one go.

The Fat Caramba lost his way and made straight for me. I held open the lid of my strong shoe-box and he ran straight into it. Then I shut the lid and the next day I collected the reward of four thousand, two hundred and three trouser buttons

from clockwork King January. I bought hazelnuts with them, of course. Twenty-four cases full. Thirty cases of nuts I ate up, and fourteen I sold. With the money I started a banana plantation. . . ."

At this point, Lari Fari Tricktooth the Lying Nutcracker fell asleep and dreamed all night long of a plantation with seven different kinds of nuts, and about a little hare who was his wife, and about a toy-chest land where there wasn't an Honest Lion John watching all the time to see that no lies were told.

"This time he really didn't lie," thought the Honest Lion John to himself, "for there is right, and there is left. I have got it too. Just here, by this paw, is right, and exactly opposite, is left."

9. How Lari Fari Tricktooth became the Chief Scissors-Grinder, conquered a company of tin soldiers, and how all of them tumbled into a river.

"I have over two hundred teeth on either side," said Lari Fari Tricktooth, the Lying Nutcracker, "three hundred on the right and three hundred on the left, and five hundred on top and five hundred on the bottom, too. Now that isn't a lie, honestly."

"Today I shall catch him," growled the Honest Lion John. "He seems to think that we can't count. First he says two hundred, then three hundred, and then he says five hundred. I shall keep my eye on this liar today—but tomorrow I shall let him slide right through my teeth for breakfast. He'll taste just like asparagus with melted butter."

"One tooth is sharper than the others," went on the Lying Nutcracker to his friends. "Once, for instance, I passed through a town called Stick-in-the-mud. I was on the way to India to order a load of nuts. I have always liked Indian nuts best of all, so I had decided to order two or three shiploads of them. So there I was, walking through Stick-in-the-mud, wondering why there was such a festive air and what was causing such a tremendous noise. It was even gayer than at our funfair in Suck-a-sweet. People were running backwards and forwards wearing

paper hats and blowing paper squeakers.

"Children with gingerbread men hanging round their necks were tooting on tin trumpets. Women were dressed up, and from every house came the marvellous smell of toffee making and cake baking. At every corner there were street traders selling Turkish delight and roasted almonds.

"It turned out to be the scissors-grinders' fair. The great moment of the day was the great scissors-grinding contest which took place at exactly three o'clock. Scissors-grinders had come from all over the world for it, bringing their grindstones and their gipsy wives. On the grindstones sat their monkeys, firmly attached to them.

"Now the people of Stick-in-the-mud had collected lots and lots of blunt scissors specially for the contest, so that the grinders could show how skilled they were. Well, I moved quietly around among the crowds, ate a little Turkish delight, and bought myself some nuts at a stall. But when the contest started, I went and put my name down for it. All the grinders were standing in a row in the market place, while their monkeys

grinned down from the grindstones and
their wives, all wearing their most colour-
ful skirts, stood close by.

" 'You haven't got a grindstone, and
you haven't got a gipsy wife, and you
haven't got a monkey. So how are you
going to manage?' asked the Mayor of
Stick-in-the-mud, laughing at me.

"Then the contest started. People
brought scissors. They were so blunt that
it would have been easier to teach an
elephant to play the piano without any
music than to sharpen them. Sweat
poured off the foreheads of all the

scissors-grinders. The gipsy women danced wildly round the grindstones, while their beautiful skirts billowed out and their bracelets clinked musically on their wrists—and as for the monkeys, they made as much noise as the grindstones themselves. You could hear the noise at least half a mile away.

"But *I* won the contest. At last, you see, they brought out a pair of scissors— scissors so blunt that a paper policeman could have ridden all the way to America with them, without spurs too. All the scissors-grinders worked on this pair of scissors, one after the other. The sparks flew in all directions but no one could make them sharp—until I came along. I put on my scissors-grinding teeth, held the scissors in one hand very lightly, and then pulled them through my teeth. Sssst! Once from left to right. Sssst! Once from right to left—"

"He's right this time," muttered John the Honest Lion. "Now he really isn't lying, for I have got a right and a left too."

"Those scissors became so sharp," went on Lari Fari Tricktooth, "that a flea would have been cut into two if it had

dared to balance itself on either of the blades.

"First of all, the Mayor of Stick-in-the-mud had specially to test them. He let the thread of a cobweb drift in the air, then he held the scissors up against the wind—and sssst! The thread flew away in two pieces. After that he made a general test. He asked six people to bring a tree trunk to him. He just put the scissor blades to the trunk and one half of it fell to the right and the other to the left. . . ."

"Well, I should think he's lying now," grumbled Honest John the Lion, "for if I can carry a heavy tree trunk all on my own, then why did it take six people from Stick-in-the-mud to do the same thing? But on the other hand, he isn't lying after all, for there *is* a right and there *is* a left."

"I received the Order of Merit," went on the Lying Nutcracker, "for Scissors-Sharpeners, and became the Chief Scissors-Grinder of Stick-in-the-mud.

"After that I saved the town from tin soldiers. I cannot stand soldiers. They bawl, and they sing stupid, horrible-sounding songs, and you can smell them miles away because of their stinking socks and their cannon oil. They block roads with their cars and they make a lot of noise.

"Well, the day after the competition, a man who brought vegetables into the town reported that he had seen a company of tin soldiers marching in the direction of Stick-in-the-mud, singing loudly as they tramped along. I didn't need to make a special effort. Next to the river which flows past Stick-in-the-mud— it's called the River Mud, as a matter of fact—I put my giant nutcracker set of teeth, camouflaged as a town gate. When the soldiers arrived, bawling and singing, they didn't march through the gate of the town which I had hidden under grass, but they went straight through my giant nutcracker false teeth, their lieutenant leading the way.

"Now soldiers are never allowed to do anything unless their lieutenant orders them to. Well, the lieutenant fell into the Mud. The second soldier followed and sank as well, and so did the third. The singing became fainter and fainter as fewer and fewer soldiers were left. The River Mud took them all. They were washed into the sea—and the town was saved. I marched on to India, myself, and bought my hundred shiploads full of nuts."

"Even if he *has* lied," purred the Honest Lion John, "I shan't eat him up because I liked that story. I can't bear soldiers myself."

10. How Lari Fari Tricktooth had to bite trouser buttons, and how he was rescued from a calamity.

"Do tell us a nice story about Christmas," pleaded Teddybear the Violinist. "I do so love Christmas. Once I was asked out at Christmas time, and it was then that I gave my first concert with my violin. It was so beautiful that everyone just had to cry. That's why Christmas is called Christmas, of course—it's really *Cries*-mas, coming from the word 'cries'."

"If you tell a lie," warned Honest John the Lion, "Teddybear the Violinist will have to cry again before very long—over you, this time, for I shall eat you up. Honestly!"

"Oh, yes," barked the dog with three legs and no tail, "I should like to cry too. Let Honest John eat him up."

"I don't lie," cried Lari Fari Tricktooth the Lying Nutcracker, "because I am never *not* lying. But I do know a lovely story about Christmas.

"It was at the time when I was employed as a nutcracker by a rich man who lived in his grand villa with his fat wife. They had two children. It was the day before Christmas. Now, as you all know, rich people almost always have everything worked by electricity—floor polishing, mending, sewing, knitting, cake-baking, window polishing, and even nut-cracking. It wasn't very nice for me, I can tell you, for after all, what use am I to anyone if I'm not used for cracking nuts? Well, Christmas day came. The children's presents were left around all over the place. There were electric trains and fire engines, electric talking dolls, machines like juke boxes and pin-ball tables, just like those in amusement arcades, and all working by electricity too, robots, and steamships steered by remote control. Everything was made from plastic or metal. There was nothing made of wood at all. And the food!

"There were chocolates, boxes of sweets, and forty pounds of nuts—some with gold shells, some with silver and some were just ordinary nuts. As you can imagine, after all this the father was soon completely full up, and the mother was full too, and as for the children, well, they had completely ruined their stomachs they had stuffed them so. The dog didn't want his sausage, the talking doll

was gabbling nonsense, and I was cross
about everything.

"I felt really ill that night because that
beastly boy of that awful family had put

lead pellets and trouser buttons and pebbles between my teeth, and finally he had made me bite the back of a chair. But although there were over a thousand nuts around, nobody ate any. I was glad when they all went to bed at last, because then, my friends, I was able to celebrate all by myself.

"I carried more than a hundred and ninety nuts to the window sill and put them all down in a long row, and I opened the window with my strong teeth. It was dark in the street. There was nobody about at all. Then I cracked the nuts open, one after another. When it was light, the birds flew down and I fed them. I fetched more nuts, cracked them and

put those out as well. It makes you feel good, you see, to feed the birds.

"At eleven, the people got up. When they saw what I had done, they threw me out—into the street! There I was found by the son of the chief railway signalman, Mr. Railman. He took me home with him where they let me sit by the warm stove. I was given a bowl of beechnuts and hazelnuts, and all day long I cracked them, one after another. At night they wrapped me up in a handkerchief so that I wouldn't feel cold. There were six brothers and sisters, and they always used to say, 'What a lovely nutcracker this is. It doesn't squeak either.' "

"Not a bad story," said the broken dog with three legs and no tail, "but it hasn't made me cry."

"It's true, though," said Teddybear the Fiddler. "I remember exactly. I lived at that time with chief railway signalman Mr. Railman, and one day his son Joe came to visit him and brought Lari Fari Tricktooth with him—so it isn't a lie."

"If it's not a lie, then it's the truth," growled Honest John the Lion. "But if I don't catch him lying soon, I shall die pitifully—of starvation. Honestly!"

11. How Lari Fari Tricktooth once milked oxen, and how he nearly invented a complicated cake-mixture-moving machine, and how John the Honest Lion wanted to make a meal of him.

"Once upon a time," began Lari Fari Tricktooth one evening, when they had all settled down, "I had a good job with a farmer in Bangland as a labourer. At that time I had exactly twenty-three sets of interchangeable false teeth, which was lucky for me because the farmer had exactly twenty-three oxen in his stables.

"I shall first have to tell you how I organised my work, for this is the most important thing about work for me. I have to arrange it cleverly, so that I don't overdo it and hurt my teeth too much. While everyone was asleep, I carried my twenty-three buckets into the stables and put each one in a separate stall beneath each ox. Then I attached one set of teeth to one tail, so that this way I could make each set milk each of the oxen. That's how clever I was!"

"You call that clever, eh!" growled Honest John the Lion. "Don't make me

laugh! Fancy not knowing that oxen aren't milked from their tails! Everyone knows they are milked from—milked—er—" He frowned. "I've forgotten just where they are milked from." (Of course,

Honest John wasn't right either, for oxen don't give any milk at all.) "But," he went on, "there *is* one thing I *do* know about. I know that you are going to taste just as good as you are beginning to smell. Honestly!"

"Well," said Lari Fari Tricktooth quickly, "one day there was going to be a wedding between the farmer's son, Walter, and the daughter of Farmer Bullock—but it nearly didn't take place. They invited several hundred guests and they had started to make the wedding cake. It was so large that they had to mix it in a hundred different washtubs. Somehow something went wrong. Somebody put too much yeast in. You all know what yeast does. When the cake or the bread or whatever it is is in the oven, it makes it all rise so that instead of a cake (or bread) coming out flat like a pancake, it comes out so high and light and airy, looking like a beautiful puffball, only tasting a thousand times better.

"But somebody put all this extra yeast in and then, because it was a lovely hot day—the hottest day for years—the cake mixture started to rise and rise and rise. And then it began to overflow from the washtubs and tumbled down the sides, and over the floor, and out of the doors, and into the streets and it rolled down the roads and into the fields. It simply didn't stop. Even the market square was covered with it. The maids tried to hold it back with their brooms and then they tried to sweep it all into one place. There were mountains of it everywhere, mountains so high that you could hardly see over them. It seemed as if the wedding would just have to be called off. Then I came along!

"I lay down comfortably behind a great slippery mountain of it and. . . ."

"At home in Wetborough, a marvellous wedding was called off once," began Inky-Punch, babbling on once again, "and that was really terrible. They hadn't got a bride or a bridegroom for a start. Everyone had arrived and the baker. . . ." Teddybear rapped him smartly on the head with his bow and he quietened down once again.

The Lying Nutcracker took no notice. "There I was, comfortably settled behind this heap of cake mixture but finally I decided to lend them a hand. I made my set of giant false teeth shovel it all up and

dump it down again, so that before long
it was all collected together in one place.
So you see, I invented a cake-mixture-
moving machine. You might almost say I

invented cake mixes too. Now, you can hardly call that a lie!"

"Now I shall mix you up too, friend False Tooth," purred the Honest Lion John happily. "You take your chattering teeth out of your lying mouth and we'll give them a decent burial. *You* won't be needing them any more. I shall eat you up, bones and all. You told a lie, you know you did!" He edged nearer and caught hold of the Lying Nutcracker by his trousers and opened his mouth and—

"No, no!" cried the crocodile Bimbanfiddleraddle. "I know of a machine like that. Its front has teeth just like the nutcracker's and at the back is a mechanical shovel, and there are wheels underneath, too. I once lived in a toy-chest where there was one."

John the Honest Lion let go of the Lying Nutcracker. "Well," he sighed, "if that's true, then it isn't a lie. Sometimes I think to myself that he lies and sometimes I think that he doesn't. He'll drive me stark staring mad one day, really he will. Honestly!"

"Well, then," admitted the Lying Nutcracker, "perhaps I only *nearly* invented a cake-mechanical-machine-shovel-mix, only it was one without wheels. But you must agree that I half invented it, at least. Now, you can't really call that a lie!"

And Lari Fari Tricktooth planned to tell a story the next time about horse racing.

12. This is a story in which Lari Fari Tricktooth won the first prize in a trotting race—without a horse.

"A long time ago I used to have some false teeth that were very fond of horses —little horses, big horses, black horses, brown horses, white horses, piebald horses, horses made from wood, and horses made from marzipan. In short, they loved all the horses in the world— but I didn't know that at the time, and so, all unsuspecting, I went to the horse races. People let me go right to the front by the railings. . . ."

"I've nearly caught him lying now," growled the Honest Lion John, "for there are only railings on ships. But still a stupid lie like this is no more than a little one. I'll catch him properly with a big one later on!"

"Everyone knew me, for I was as famous as any singer—pop, opera, rock or roll. There I stood. The horses with their carts behind them were at the starting line. Each cart had two wheels and a driver, and as soon as the referee gave the signal to start, the horses raced off, galloping along the course dragging their

carts along, while the drivers held on to the reins. Then, my friends, something happened!

"I had only cracked two nuts with my brand-new exchangeable false teeth when they tore themselves away from me and ran after the horses. I just managed to catch hold of the last tooth. My other hand, as it happened, gripped something that turned out to be a rein. My false teeth raced after the horses and we had done half a lap before I managed to harness the reins to the teeth and then I hung on for grim death. And how they ran! They ran and ran, and soon they caught up with the other horses and even came into fourth place.

"I heard the spectators shout, 'Lari Fari Tricktooth! Put your money on Lari

Fari Tricktooth!' You see, people always bet on which horse is going to win and they bet money on it. Whoever wins is the winner, of course. And who won that race? I did! I got the first prize. We were the first to finish—and all the people who put their money on me were winners too. Now, it isn't a lie!"

"He who wins is the winner," growled Honest John the Lion. "That's true. And if that is true, then he hasn't told a lie—but if he had told one, then I would have eaten him up without a second thought. Honestly!"

13. How Ları Fari Tricktooth saved the lives of the clockwork King January and his daughter, and also that of the electric Lord Hick de Hupp and became Minister for Nuts as a reward.

"I really like telling stories where my wedding comes ın, or stories about horses best," said the Lying Nutcracker, "and so I'm going to tell you one in which both of them are mentioned together. It's all about my marvellous wedding celebrations and four fiery horses.

"At that time I was living in the toy-chest country of Suck-a-sweet. Our emperor was clockwork King January who was wound up by his tiny crown. His daughter was the clockwork Princess Wilhelmina Powder-compact who could be taken apart. Everything about her was movable. Now one day there was going to be a lovely wedding, for the beautiful princess was going to be married to the electric Lord Hick de Hupp (who had a five-volt battery in his back). Even then he was a bit damaged, and so he kept on getting attacks of hiccups. The princess, however, was supposed to marry him just the same.

"Now all this happened on a Sunday. We had a three-piece band. The velvet monkey blew his trumpet in the front, and behind him came the clown with his accordion, and in the rear was the drumming bear. A little sugar doll who could say 'Mama' sang with them.

"Four horses pulled the coach. A pair were side by side, harnessed together, and behind them were another pair. On the top sat Fidgetty Punch who acted as coachman. More than a hundred toy people had travelled from various toychests for the occasion. The clockwork King January, wearing his tin crown with the winder in it, had already distributed three bags of sweets. I myself cracked over a hundred sacks of nuts which were

to be given to poor wooden birds. It looked like being a really riotous feast— and then something happened."

"Sometimes," pondered Honest John the Lion to himself, "I think that he cannot crack nuts at all, for he who talks a lot has no work. And he who has no work has no nuts either. I shall look for a hard nut in our toy-chest tomorrow, and he will have to crack it. If he doesn't, then I shall eat him up! Honestly!"

"And then something happened," continued the Lying Nutcracker. "It was something terribly dangerous. I told you that the velvet monkey was in front blowing his trumpet, didn't I? Well, that was fun, but at the back the bear beat his drum too loudly and so suddenly the horses reared up and raced off. The Fidgetty Punch fell off the coachbox and landed squirming, right on top of the sugar doll. She gasped and cried, 'Mama! Mama-ma!' Then the wild horses bolted and galloped down the road. Everything rolled about. The clockwork king and his beautiful daughter who were in the coach began to make clockwork movements and to tremble, while the electric Lord Hick de Hupp got a violent attack of hiccups. The horses ran round in mad circles. Talk about a fine how-d'ye do! Nobody dared to get anywhere near those fiery steeds—but then I came along!

"I put my fox-catching false teeth behind the drum and I stood myself behind the strong monkey with the gorgeous velvet admiral's hat. Like that, you see, I couldn't be spotted by the horses. It was a sensible thing to do, for if they had caught me I would have finished up looking like mashed potato. It's no good trying to catch wild horses with understanding—you need cunning. So when they rushed past again and started to hurtle round the drum, my fox-trappers snapped tight and caught them by the reins, pulling them back and making them stand still.

"While clockwork King January was still rattling around in the coach and the beautiful Princess Powder-compact cried, for she had come to pieces, poor electric Lord Hick de Hupp hicked and hupped constantly until he could go on no longer, for his battery was all used up.

"In spite of all this, the wedding did take place after all, for I was made the bridegroom. I managed to put all the pieces of the Princess Powder-compact together again. And so the feast was able to go on after all. It was a fabulous wedding. After it, I became the Minister of

Nuts and sat on the left of the clockwork King January of the toy-chest country. Honestly!" At this point Lari Fari Tricktooth showed his left side as if by doing so he could prove that it was all true.

The Honest Lion John growled, "Just then I really thought that I could have eaten him—but left is left. That's right enough, and what is right can't be wrong. And after all, left is here by my right paw. I can feel that myself. That villain has been lucky, though. I would have eaten him without any ceremony at all if he'd lied. Honestly!"

14. How Lari Fari Tricktooth went on a
    steamer at Plum Whitsun, was eaten
    by a lion, but finished up by defeat-
    ing the lion after all.

"At Plum Whitsun," Lari Fari Tricktooth
the Lying Nutcracker began, "I used to
enjoy going away. Mostly I went into the
mountains to pick flowers, but once I
went to India. . . ."

"I know," Inky-Punch babbled, "when
it's Plum Whitsun. It's when it's Easter—
no, I mean, when the plums grow at
Whitsun, because whenever. . . ."

At this point the Fiddler Teddybear
promptly hit him on the nose with his
bow, and said, "You don't have to tell us
that. Every child here knows it. Now
don't interrupt the lovely story!"

As Inky-Punch fell silent, the Lying
Nutcracker went on. "Well, I went to
India because I wanted to hunt lions."

Honest Lion John let him go for a bit.
"The more he says," he thought to himself, "the more lies he will tell. Perhaps
he won't even have time to take his boots
off for it would take far too long. I shall
eat him up, just as he is. Honestly!"

"Well, the steamer to India always

leaves at 6.23 sharp from the Duck-pond."

"Second lie," said the Honest Lion John, counting carefully. "The steamer doesn't start at the Duckpond."

"A steamer trip is fun, because you can always look at a lot of seagulls—but it is dangerous, too. As it happened, we froze fast in the ice half-way across the ocean. Frost had turned all the water into thick, thick ice. The ship couldn't move an inch either backwards or forwards.

"Well, we on board thought to ourselves, 'Frost comes and frost goes,' and so we made ourselves comfortable and played cards. It wasn't any good, though, because the frost didn't go. We stuck fast in the ice for so long that the first penguins began to go past us. They always walk from the North Pole to the

South Pole for their summer holidays."

"Third lie," noted John the Honest Lion. "At the South Pole it is just as cold as the North Pole. I once had a polar bear for a friend. I know all about it through him."

"We played every card game we could think of at least a hundred times," Lari Fari Tricktooth went on, "and our rations were beginning to come to an end. The sailors were absolutely freezing and it looked as if they were about to mutiny—and that's where I came in! I fixed my stone-crushing teeth to the bows of the steamer, the captain gave the order, the mate spun the wheel, and then my stone-crushing teeth ground up the ice without the slightest bit of trouble. We sailed off in the direction of India and there, waiting for me, was my friend Ibn-Bubbub Boon, the Emir."

"Fourth lie," counted the Honest Lion. "There are no Emirs in India. Emirs live in Arabia."

"Emir Ibn-Bubbub Boon carried his famous Winchester rifle with him—fully automatic, it was, with eleven bullets already in the magazine, so there was no need to reload. I myself," said Lari Fari

Tricktooth, "always fight without a gun. I don't think it's very sporting behaviour to carry on like that with lions. A lion only has his keen intelligence to fight with, while a hunter has an automatic rifle."

"With his keen intelligence," repeated Honest John the Lion, "that's true—but if it's true, then he isn't telling a lie. And if he's not telling lies then I can't eat him up. He's driving me quite mad. Sometimes I think he's telling lies, and sometimes I think that he isn't—"

"We took the shortest route to the jungle," went on Lari Fari Tricktooth, "because I had lost a lot of time through the frost and my Plum Whitsun holidays were coming to an end. First of all we came to the prairie. The grass grows higher than your head there. Then we went through the marshes where there were a hundred dangers lurking, and then we came to the middle of the jungle. I walked ahead because I was stronger, and behind me came Ibn-Bubbub Boon. We stalked the lions, keeping them to windward, but the lions, who were far from stupid, had seen us approaching for ages, and they were themselves following us

from behind, keeping *us* to windward, too.

"At the head of them was the biggest and the most dangerous, with the biggest and sharpest teeth and the softest paws. He could creep up so quietly that not even a midge could hear him. Well, he came nearer and nearer behind us—and then he snapped at the Winchester rifle with his teeth, snatched it out of the hands of my friend, and swallowed it! Lions are far from stupid, as I've already said!"

"He's right about that," growled John the Honest Lion. "I'm certainly not stupid. If you tell one lie—just one lie, my friend—I shall spot it straight away, and then. . . ."

"Lions *are* clever," the Lying Nutcracker went on, "and so he must have thought to himself that if the rifle was gone then the hunter must have become as weak as a fly—and he was right. At that moment I turned round. The Emir Ibn-Bubbub Boon was as good as lost. The lion was already licking his lips."

"So am I!" cried Honest John the Lion joyfully. "Today I shall catch him out. If he tells a lie about a lion then I'll show him no mercy."

Lari Fari Tricktooth picked up the thread of his story again. "For the first time I saw my friend afraid. He thought his last moment had come. But that was where I came in. I leapt between him and the lion and I allowed myself to be eaten."

"Now I've caught you, you Lying Nutcracker," growled John the Honest Lion. "Someone who has been eaten—and eaten by a lion at that—has vanished from the face of the earth for ever. Honestly!

Come here, brother nutcracker! Let us shake hands and say goodbye before I make a meal of you." Then Honest John went over to the nutcracker, licked his lips and held out his paw to say goodbye.

However, Lari Fari Tricktooth said to him, "I shall prove to you that I'm not telling lies. Just wait a minute, Honest John. I only let myself be eaten because I knew that a lion can never be conquered. Is that right?"

"Of course it is," growled Honest John the Lion. "It's true, and what is true is no lie."

"Well, then, since a lion can't be conquered from the outside, I carried out the job from the inside. I took the rifle, pressed the trigger, and killed the lion with just one shot. My friend Ibn-Bubbub Boon was already blubbing behind some bushes where he had hidden, thinking it was all up with me and that he would never see me again—and then the lion fell down." Lari Fari Tricktooth talked faster and faster in an excited way, for he was afraid that the Honest Lion John really would eat him up. "Fell—fell down, conquered from inside by me."

"That's a lie," hissed the Honest Lion furiously. "A lion is unconquerable."

"But it isn't a lie," cried the Lying Nutcracker. "Look, I can prove it. Can you not see me, Honest John?"

"Of course I can see you," growled the Honest Lion.

"You aren't telling a lie, are you?" Lari Fari Tricktooth asked him.

"I have never, never told you a lie," said Honest John.

"Then it is true!" cried the Lying Nutcracker. "And what is true is not a lie. You said that yourself."

"He gets me all mixed up," grumbled Honest John the Lion. "I don't know myself what is true and what isn't. But if

I ever catch him lying I shall certainly eat him up, just as he is—boots, hat, wood-worm and all. Honestly!"